I ~~can't~~ can fly

Fifi Kuo

Boxer Books

Little Penguin
wanted to fly
like other birds.

"Why can't I fly?" asked Little Penguin.

"Ha!" said Gull. "Penguins CAN'T fly!"

"But I do have wings," thought Little Penguin.

So Little Penguin
flapped.

Then flapped
some more.

Then flapped
really hard.

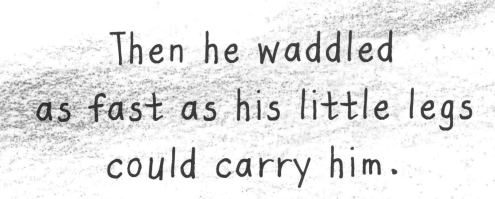

Then he waddled
as fast as his little legs
could carry him.

And he leapt . . .

and
whoosh,
splat...

He landed
in front
of his dad.

"What are
you doing,
Little Penguin?"
asked Dad.

"I want to fly!"
said Little Penguin.

"Like
other
birds."

"Penguins can't fly,"
said Dad.
"Penguins swim."

"I'm sure I can fly,"
thought Little Penguin.

So Little Penguin flipped and flapped
his little wings.

And flipped

and flapped some more.

Little Penguin was exhausted.

"I can do better,"
said Little Penguin.

Then he slipped,

and slipped,

bumped

and tripped
and . . .

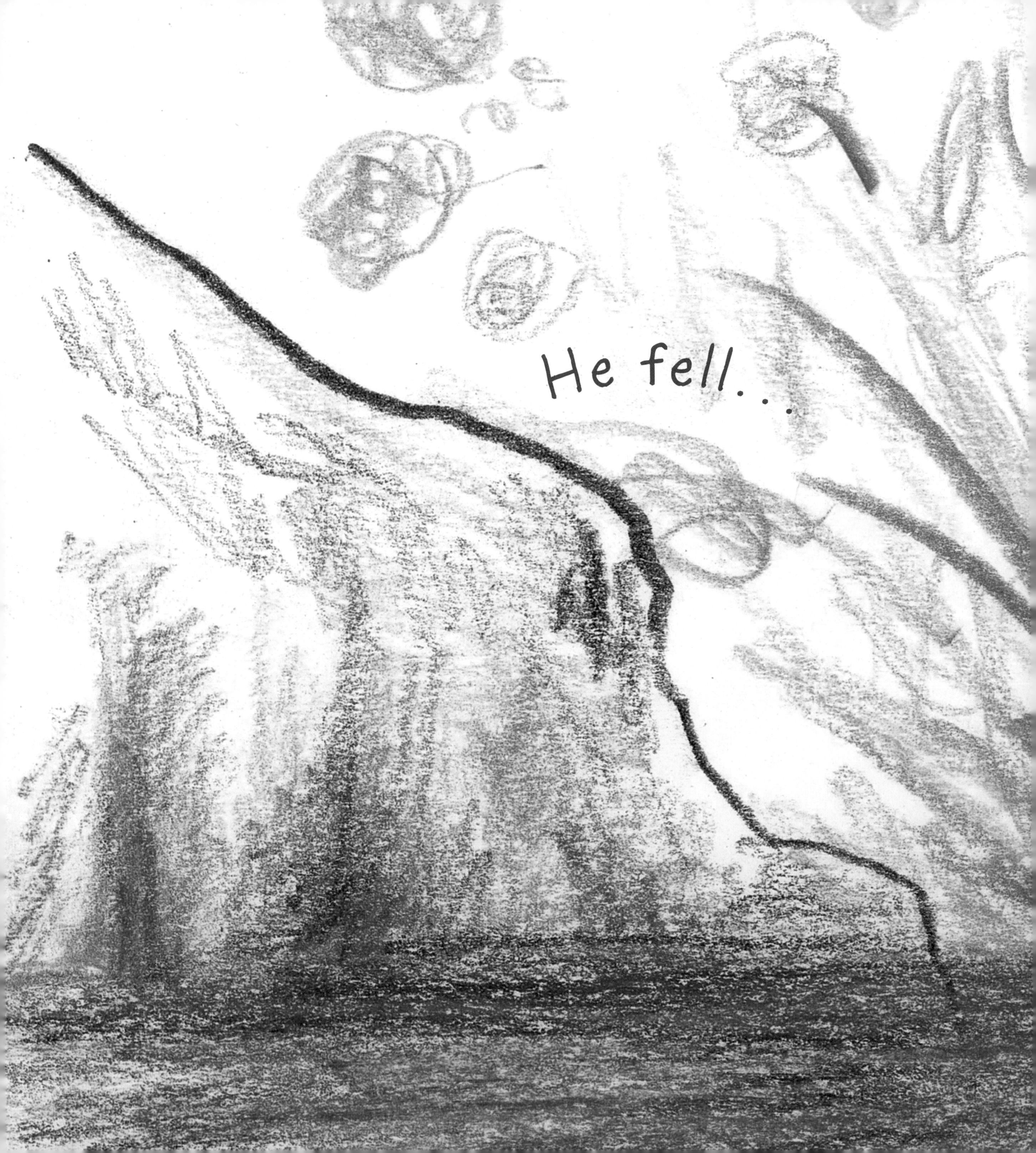

He fell...

SPLASH!

into the sea.

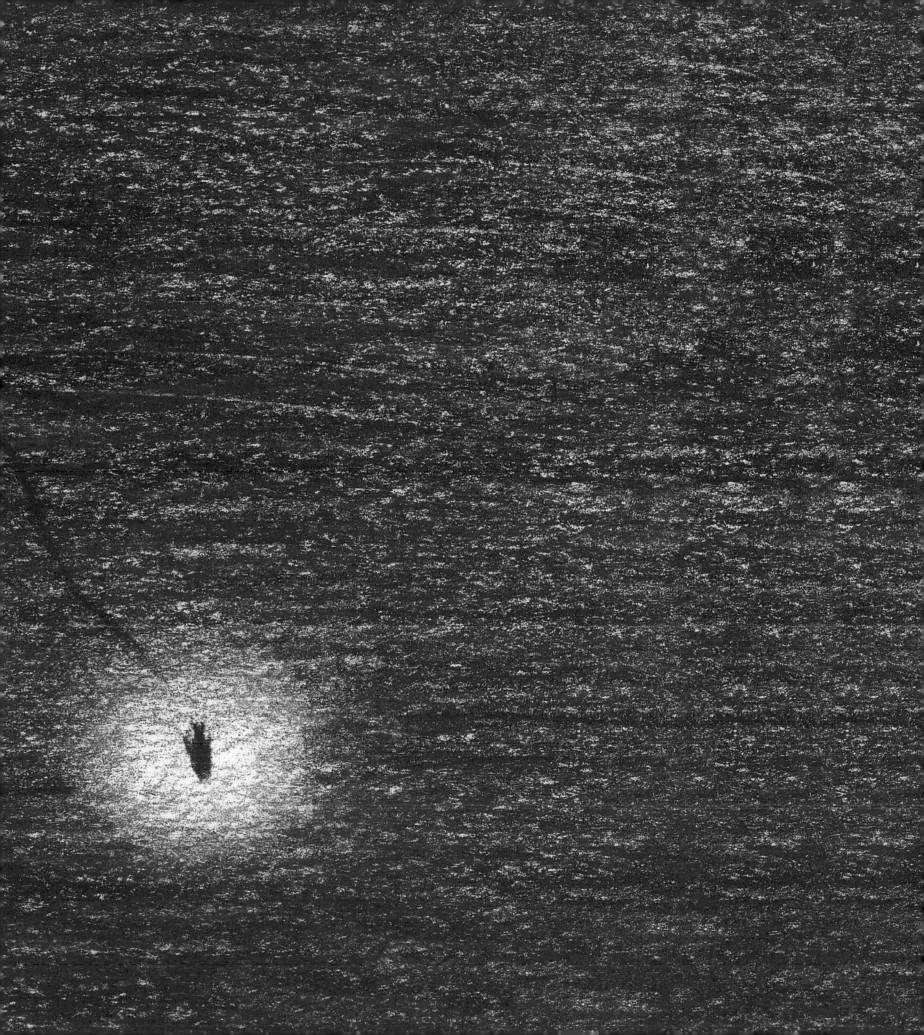

Dad was close by

and took Little Penguin's wing.

They swam below the sea.
They leapt above the sea.

They flew in the air
and dived again and again.

"This is just like flying," thought Little Penguin.

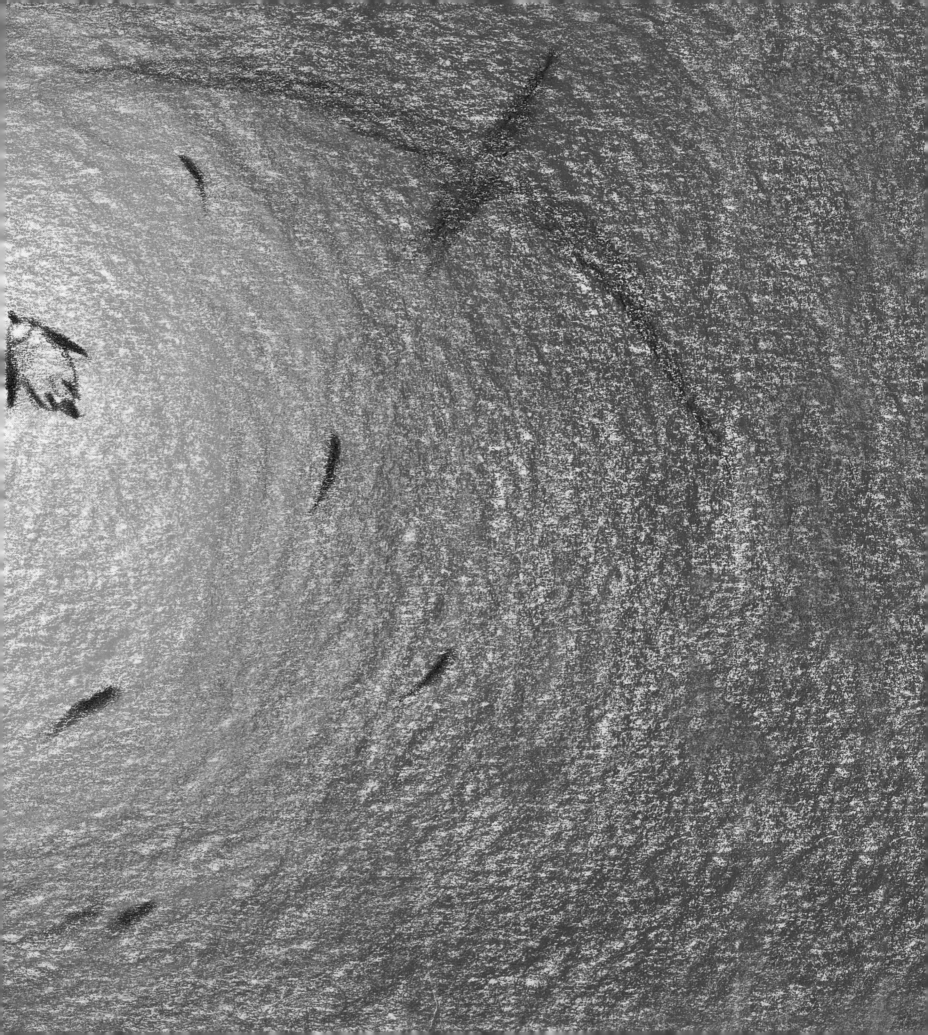

"Swimming is like flying,
isn't it, Dad?"

"Almost the same, my little penguin."

"I can fly!"

This book is for my parents and grandparents
for giving me the chance to have adventures.
For Martin, Caroline, David and Leilani
thanks for believing that I can fly.
Thank you too, to my Godparents in Chung-Li, Lynn, Enoch, and my friends,
who always cheer me up. And you, who are reading this book.
Fifi Kuo

First published in Great Britain in 2018 by Boxer Books Limited.
This paperback edition first published in 2020 by Boxer Books Limited.
www.boxerbooks.com
Boxer® is a registered trademark of Boxer Books Limited.

A catalogue record for this book is available from the British Library.
The illustrations were prepared using charcoal and digital colour.
The text is set in Kristenalwaysnotsonormal.

ISBN 978 1 912757 61 9

1 3 5 7 9 10 8 6 4 2

Printed in China

All of our papers are sourced from managed forests and renewable resources.